Our Little Norman Cousin of Long Ago

This edition published 2026
by Living Book Press
Copyright © Living Book Press, 2026

ISBN: 978-1-76183-140-9 (hardcover)
        978-1-76183-139-3 (softcover)

First published in 1915.

A catalogue record for this
book is available from the
National Library of Australia

Our little Norman cousin of long ago

by

Evaleen Stein

Henri
Alan

Contents

1.	An Invitation	1
2.	The Castle of Noireat	11
3.	Rolf the Ganger	18
4.	Blanchette and Marie	25
5.	"The Mystery of the Rivers"	35
6.	Little Duke Richard	45
7.	The Tournament	56
8.	Old Herve Tells Another Story	65
9.	Hugh Becomes a Knight	74
10.	On the Way to Dives	82
11.	Waiting for the Wind	94
12.	The Duchess Matilda's Gift	101

CHAPTER I

An Invitation

It was a May morning in Normandy in the year 1066, and through all the grassy valleys the pear and apple trees were clouds of white and rosy bloom. Some of them overhung the little thatched huts of the peasant folk, which stood close together making the tiny village of Noireat; and some of the flowery trees clambered up the slopes of the steep limestone cliff that rose behind the village. Crowning this cliff was the great gray castle of Count Bertram, the lord of Noireat.

Within the walls of the castle was a large courtyard, where two boys were playing ball. Each was dressed in a tunic of dark green cloth; that is, a close-fitting garment belted at the waist and with a scant skirt reaching to just above the knee; on the boys' legs were long black hose and on their feet shoes of thick soft leather without heels and with long pointed toes; on their heads were little caps, each with a black cock's feather stuck into a buckle at one side.

Presently, "Hark, Alan!" cried one of the boys, "I thought I heard a trumpet!"

Both lads paused in their play; then as they caught clearly another shrill blast, "Come, Henri," said Alan, "let us go to the battlements and see who is coming!"

Off they scampered across the courtyard, through a narrow doorway in a strong tower near the gate of the castle and up a winding flight of stone steps that led to the top of the wall. This wall, which inclosed the castle, and to which parts of it were joined, was very thick and strong; and in a small tower over the gate-way stood a man-at-arms whose duty it was to watch all who came thither, and, if foes, to warn the lord so that he might make ready to defend himself. For in those days nobleman often made war on one another and people who lived in castles expected to keep constant watch for enemies.

But they were quite often friends as foes who rode along the steep bridle path to Noireat; for people played almost as much as they fought, and liked entertainment as well as we do to-day.

As Alan and Henri reached the top step of the winding stair, the man-at-arms, who had been gazing down at the bridle path, turned, and said with a smile, "Well, youngsters. I think we may look for one of those play fights that folks call tourneys. I'll wager yonder horseman are coming to invite Count Bertram, for they are heralds of his friend the Baron of Brecey. Do you see that zig-zag green band and the three red spots worked on the little flags hanging from their trumpets? That is the device of the Baron of Brecey."

The lads looked eagerly down at the two riders who were by this time quite near the gate-way, and, sure enough, they could make out the embroidery of which the watchman spoke.

"I don't think that device is so handsome as the red two-legged dragon on Count Bertram's flag," said Alan critically.

"Why does he have that dragon on his flag, and his shield, too?" asked Henri.

"Well," answered the watchman, rubbing his forehead, "I don't exactly know. Maybe Count Bertram, or some of his kinfolks, fought a red two-legged dragon somewhere, or maybe he just liked its looks. I don't know either whether there is any particular meaning to those spots and things the Baron of Brecey has. But it's a good thing for a knight to have *some* kind of device."

"Why is it?" asked Alan.

"Why, there is a reason for it, youngster," said the watchman, "and it's this; when they go to fight in war or those play-battle tourneys or tournaments, or whatever they call them, their faces and bodies are so covered up by the armor they have to wear to protect themselves, that no one can tell who they are unless they have a device somewhere about them, painted on their shields or worked on their banners. And as most of the knights know the devices of the rest, it is about as good as having one's name told to everybody. The trouble is though that they don't all stick to the same device they pick out, but a good many of them change it sometimes when they take a notion to, and that gets people mixed up about their names."

"Count Bertram always has the red two-legged dragon," said Henri.

"Yes," replied the watchman, "and he says that by and by all the knights will have to settle on regular devices and hand them down in their families, so people can always be sure who they are.—And maybe they will," he added.

But while Alan and Henri had been talking with the watchman, the heralds had reached the gate of the castle where they halted and each blew another shrill blast on his trumpet.

At this the lads, with eyes dancing, turned about and racing down the stairs and back to the courtyard joined a group of younger boys, all, like themselves, pages in the household. Indeed, everybody in the castle had come into the courtyard by this time, from Count Bertram, the lord of Noireat and Lady Gisla, his wife, down to the cooks and scullions; for visitors were few, and if they came on peaceful errands were always warmly welcomed.

Meantime Master Herve, the gate-keeper, opened the heavy door at the end of an arched passage under the watch-tower and let down the narrow drawbridge that was held up by ropes to the castle wall. Outside the wall was the moat, a ditch filled with water deep enough to drown any one who tried to ride through it; and the drawbridge was so called because it could be drawn up and folded against the wall until the gate-keeper knew whether it was friend or foe who wished to enter.

As now the two horsemen rode into the courtyard of Noireat, a pair of little pages hurried out and held their bridles while Alan and Henri helped them dismount. One of the heralds then blew a third blast on his trumpet as the other, taking his place on the high curb of a well near by and raising his voice, called out "My master, the Baron of Brecey, sends greeting to the Count of Noireat and his household, and proclaims a tourney to be held four weeks from to-day in the meadow adjoining his castle, and he invites all Norman knights who so desire to contest for the prizes, which will be a pair of gilded spurs for the first champion and a silver hunting-horn for him adjudged second winner!"

When he had finished, everybody clapped their hands; and "Oh Henri," whispered Alan, "do you suppose Count Bertram will take us along?"

"I'm sure I hope so!" answered Henri.

"What is a tourney?" asked one of the little pages, in a low voice, as he clung tightly to the bridle of the herald's horse.

"Why," said Henri, with a superior air, for he had been to one, "it is a kind of game where knights ride on horseback and fight for fun. Their lances aren't sharp, and they don't try to kill each other, but only to see which is the best fighter, and he gets a prize. The most beautiful lady there gives it to him. And there are always lots of ladies go, for somebody has to look on, you know, and most all the men are doing the fighting."

"Oh," said the little page, with round eyes, "I wish I could go!"

"You probably can't, though," said Henri. "You are too little."

At this tears sprang to the eyes of the little page, who was only seven years old and very homesick for the castle of Briouze, which was his real home and from which he had lately been brought to Noireat. "Oh," he sobbed, "I wish I was home! Father would let me go! I don't see why everybody has to live in somebody else's house, anyway! I don't know why I had to come here!" and he began to cry in good earnest.

"There," said Henri, taking the bridle from his shaking little hand, "don't cry! You must be here, because your father is a vassal of Count Bertram. So is my father and Alan's and all the other pages'. That's why we're here, too. And I'm twelve and have been here five years. You'll like it when you get used to it: —isn't everybody good to you?"

"Y-e-s," sobbed the little page, "but I want my mother!" Here his tears broke out afresh. "Why—why can't I go home?" he quavered.

"Because," said Henri severely, "you're here to be trained. You will be a page for seven years and learn to mind, and run errands, and ride a pony, and ever so many things, and then you will be a squire for seven years more, and learn how to go hunting on horseback, and to fight, and lots more things, and then, if you have behaved right, when you are twenty-one you will be made a knight!" and Henri's eyes sparkled as he added, "And just think how grand that will be! You will have your own war-horse and armor and spurs and lance and banner and can ride out and go where you please and fight and have all kinds of adventures!" For in those days this was a gentleman's idea of life; it seldom entered their heads to do any real work in the world.

But the poor little seven-year-old was not to be comforted, and crept off to a corner of the courtyard still sobbing, "I want my mother! I want to go home! I don't see why people are other people's vassals! I don't want to be a page! Boo-hoo-hoo!"

And it did seem strange that most of the gently born children of that time had to be brought up in "somebody else's house," as the little page complained. To understand how it came about you must know, to begin with, that the ruler of Normandy was called the duke; that the people were divided into three classes; first, the nobles who lived in castles, and, next to the duke, were of highest rank; second, the people who lived in towns and worked at trades and kept shops and inns for travelers; and the third, or lowest class, who were poor peasants little better than slaves, and who lived in little huts in the country where they had to farm the land for the nobles. Most of the land was owned by these nobles and they, too, were of different degrees of rank, some having stronger castles than others and more fighting men under them. As a great deal of fighting was always going on, it followed that each weaker noble wanted the help and protection of some one more powerful than he was. In order to get his he must become a vassal; that is, he must promise to be loyal to his overlord, to fight for him in return, and in time of war to furnish him men and supplies. In this way it had come about that everybody in Normandy was the vassal of some one else, and it became the custom for children to be sent to their father's overlord that they might be brought up in his home and trained to be loyal to him. The lord and lady of every castle became foster parents to the boys and girls sent to them and did their best to be kind to them and to teach them all they could.

Count Bertram and Lady Gisla took a real interest in the group of squires and pages at Noireat and were much beloved in return. And now, as the little page still sobbed in his corner, Lady Gisla noticed him and a pitying look came into her eyes. "Poor little man!" she murmured to herself. Then turning to two little girls who, hand in hand, had been standing near by watching things, "Blanchette," she said, "go over to little Josef and bring him to me!"

"Yes, mother!" answered the little girl, as she ran off to do Lady Gisla's bidding.

Blanchette was the only child of Count Bertram and Lady Gisla; and though her companion, Marie, was the daughter of one of the Count's vassals, and been sent to

Noireat to be trained, Blanchette herself had stayed in her own home because Count Bertram's overlord lived in a castle near the sea where the winters were so sharp and cold that Lady Gisla feared for the health of the little girl who had been delicate since babyhood. Moreover, it was not thought so important to send girls away from home as the boys who must be trained to fight loyally, if need be, for their overlord.

In a moment Blanchette led little Josef, still sobbing, to Lady Gisla, who taking him in her arms hugged and kissed him just as his own mother might have done. "There, there!" she whispered softly to him as she dried his eyes. "Never mind! You must learn to be a little man, and we are all going to help you!" And then she kissed him again and comforted him, till presently the little page was smiling through his tears and ran along quite happily when Blanchette and Marie too him off between them to romp with one of the big brown dogs, who were barking in the general excitement caused by the coming of the heralds.

CHAPTER II

THE CASTLE OF NOIREAT

Meantime the cooks and scullions had all hurried back to their work, and as dinner was nearly ready Count Bertram invited the heralds into the castle; to be sure it was only eleven o'clock, but that was the usual hour for the midday meal.

The Count and Lady Gisla both looked very handsome as they led the way up a flight of steps to the door of the great square tower of stone, called the keep, which was the main part of the castle. Count Bertram was dressed in a tunic of dark crimson and over his black hose narrow strips of green cloth were criss-crossed up to his knees where they were tied in knots with fringed ends; his pointed leather shoes were dark crimson and so was his cap and the short mantle fastened over one shoulder with a silver clasp. Lady Gisla wore a gown of violet-colored cloth with close bodice and flaring sleeves, and her long skirt was caught up in front by a silken girdle from which hung a number of silver keys; on her head was a pointed cap, and a square of lace fastened to its peak partly covered her hair which fell over her shoulders in loose flowing locks.

Within the keep was one huge room called the hall. Heavy stone pillars upheld the floor of an upper story, and high up in the thick walls were long, narrow windows; there was no glass in these for glass was scarce and imperfect then; but sometimes in winter, when it was very cold, the windows were filled in with pieces of waxed linen instead. At either end of the room was a great fireplace; one was for warmth in winter time, while at the other the castle cooking went on the year around, for there was no other kitchen. And as there were no chimneys either, the smoke from the blazing logs, over which the cooks were busy with dinner, curled up into the hall and found its way out through the windows as best it could, which, of course, wasn't very well.

On the castle walls were no pictures, but here and there hung large pieces of cloth so skillfully embroidered that they looked almost like pictures, and here and there were fastened the antlers of a stag or a bow and sheaf of arrows. Rushes were strewn over the stone floor which was raised a little at one side of the room and called the dais. Here serving–men were placing long boards over some wooden trestles, this making a table for the lord and lady. Others were arranging a similar but much longer one down the length of the hall. There were no cloths on either of these tables, for nobody had any; and as for forks, folks expected their fingers to answer. Count Bertram and Lady Gisla had some silver dishes and glass cups; but on the long table for the household between each two persons was set an oblong wooden dish called a trencher, and this must do for a plate for both; their cups were pewter or else part of a cow's horn hollowed out and set in metal.

When all had taken their places on the benches that served for seats the long table was quite filled, for there were many people in the household. Besides the serving-folk, and the pages and squires and other attendants of gentle birth, often some wandering knight or minstrel or pilgrim or herald added to the company. Sever of the pages and squires, however, did not sit down with the others but stood on the dais ready to wait upon Count Bertram and Lady Gisla, for one of the first things taught to them was obedience and service.

Of the pages, Alan and Henri, who were inseparable friends, were favorites of the Count, while of the squires he preferred to be served by a youth names Hugh, who had been at Noireat a number of years and was now almost ready for knighthood. These three now busied themselves to attend their master, while others of their number served Lady Gisla and the little girls who sat beside her.

Henri had already been to the well in the courtyard and filled a sliver pitcher and now he brought also a silver basin, and after Count Bertram was seated at the table he poured the water over his hands into the basin and then presented him a small linen towel on which to dry them.

Meantime, Alan had gone to the kitchen end of the great hall. Here the cooks were busy at the big smoky fireplace dishing up food cooked in the copper kettles and saucepans which they pulled to the hearth from the glowing coals. On a long spit in front of the fire were pieces of roasted meat, and on either side tired little dogs were lying hungrily sniffing the food they dared not touch till their own turn came.

Each dog had a little chain fastened around his body, one end of the chain being hooked to the spit, and for almost an hour they had been obliged to walk back and forth, thus turning the spit and keeping the meat from burning. For that was the way dogs had to help cook in those days.

"How are you, Bowser? How are you, Towser?" (perhaps those were not their real names, but never mind) said Alan, as he gently poked with his foot, first one and then the other of the dogs as he waited for the cook to place some meat on the silver platter he had brought.

Henri, too, now came to the kitchen fireplace, and "There is a dish of pigeons for you to bring," said Alan as he went off with his platter.

When he set it before Count Bertram, "Where is the carving knife?" asked Hugh, who was standing by ready to carve the meat, which was one of the duties of a squire.

"Oh, dear!" cried Alan, flushing, "I never can remember that knife!" And off he hurried to the kitchen so fast that he nearly ran into Henri and his pigeons. When the knife was brought, Hugh, holding the meat firmly with a wooden skewer, carefully carved it, the two boys watching intently as he did it.

"That's right," said Count Bertram, "see how he does it, lads! Hugh will soon be a knight and go away, and then, by and by, I will expect my new squires, Alan and Henri, to do my carving,"

When the meat was served the boys brought dishes of beans, cabbage, turnips and other vegetables, but no potatoes, for the very good reason that none grew in Normandy as yet. Along with these they brought also the cake and custard and sweet things, which people then ate any time they pleased during the meal instead of keeping them for dessert as we would.

BROUGHT DISHES OF BEANS, CABBAGE,
TURNIPS AND OTHER VEGETABLES.

When Count Bertram had risen from his seat, the two pages went to the long table in the center of the hall where they found places side by side with a wooden trencher between them.

When everybody had finished eating, very likely a number of bones had been flung under the table; and it is quite possible, too, that some of the brown dogs had crept up from the kitchen hearth or the courtyard, and lying on the rumpled-up rushes munched and gnawed to their hearts' content. For people in those days were not such particular housekeepers as we are.

CHAPTER III

ROLF THE GANGER

After dinner the two heralds took their leave. Alan and Henri followed them to the gate, and when it was shut they loitered awhile in the small rood under the watch-tower where Master Herve, the gate-keeper, lived. He was an old man, and the boys liked to hear the stories he was always ready to tell.

"Well, lads," he said, as they seated themselves on a bench by the door, " 'tis lucky for you that you will get to see one more tourney before our noble ruler, Duke William, sets sail for Britain, for 'tis likely times will be dull enough with all the good knights following him across the sea!"

"Master Herve," said Henri, "why is Duke William going to fight in Britain?"

"Why, child," answered Master Herve, "the blood of Rolf the Ganger runs in his veins, and every true North-man loves a good ship and a good fight!—especially if there is a good prize at the end of it!"

"Tell us about Rolf the Ganger!" put in Alan; for

though the boys had heard the story often before, they always liked to listen to tales of their Northmen forefathers.

Master Herve smiled approvingly, and began: "Rolf, you know, was the great-great-great-grandfather of our Duke William, and was born nearly two hundred years ago on an isle off the coast of Norway. When he grew up he was so big and tall that he scorned to ride any of the little horses they have in Norway, and because he always walked instead people called him Rolf the Ganger, which means Rolf the Walker."

"And afterwhile he was outlawed!" said Henri.

"Yes," said Master Herve, "he was a wild blade, and for some deed he did he was made an outlaw by the King of Norway. But that didn't daunt Rolf the Ganger! He just got together a band of men and some dragon ships, for the men of Norway have always been famous rovers and more at home on sea than on land."

"I wish I could see a dragon ship!" exclaimed Alan longingly. "Do you think there will be some at Dives when Duke William sails for Britain next fall? You know when Count Bertram goes to join him we are to go, too, as far as Dives."

"Well," answered Herve, "the ships now are a good deal the same, only larger, and not so gay and fine looking. Rolf's were long and narrow with a high prow of wood carved like a dragon and gilded and painted in brave colors. And each had a sail of red and blue, and at the top of the mast flew a flag with a big black raven worked on it; there were dozens of long oars, too, and the shields of the warriors all glittering with red and blue and gold hung over the sides of the ships. It must have been a gallant sight to see their sails spread and the great gold dragons gliding over the curling green waves!" Here old Herve's eyes kindled as he went on, "The isle where Rolf was born was cold and bleak; so, when he started off he set his sails for the south and by and by he came to the mouth of the river Seine in the French country. Many of the Northmen sea-rovers had come to the French country before Rolf and fought the people and carried off rich booty."

And here old Herve's eyes flashed again; for though to-day we would call such doings the work of pirates, in the days of our story everybody thought it very fine and brave to get property by fighting other people and taking theirs away.

"So," went on Herve, "when the French fold saw the ships of Rolf the Ganger, they were terribly frightened, and the French King, —you remember his name, lads?" asked Herve.

"Yes," laughed the boys, "he was called Charles the Simple!"

"Right!" said Herve, "he was a very silly king, and silliest of all if he thought he could drive out the Northmen if they had once made up their minds to stay. And this they had, for Rolf's men had brought their wives and children with them, and Rolf himself had conquered the French Count of Bayeaus and married his daughter Popa and was quite ready to settle down in our beautiful Norman land, —though it wasn't called Normandy yet."

"Master Herve," interrupted Henri, "didn't Rolf's wife have any other name but Popa? You know that is just a little doll!" (For so the word means in the Norman language.)

"I daresay she did," answered Herve, "but nobody knows what it was. She must have been a pretty little thing, and a great pet to get a nickname like that, and nobody will ever call her anything but Popa, if she *was* Duke William's great-great-great-grandmother!—Well, as I was saying, Rolf's plan to settle down in the French country, while it suited him exactly, didn't suit Charles the Simple at all; and he got an army together and fought Rolf, but Rolf beat him.

"After this King Charles thought best to try and make friends with the Northmen. So he sent word to Rolf that if he would stop making war on him, and would be his friend and vassal and become a Christian (for the Northmen all worshiped old heathen gods then), he would give him all the land he had over-run, and that Rolf should be the ruler and called Duke of the Northmen, or Normans, as they soon came to be known.

"Rolf decided that he would agree to the King's terms, and in token of his promise knelt down and put his hands between the hands of King Charles and vowed he would be his faithful vassal and friend. But when he was told that at the end of the ceremony it was the custom for a vassal to kiss the foot of the King, Rolf said nothing."

Here Alan and Henri, who had been listening attentively, went off into bursts of laughter, for they knew what was coming next in the story; and old Herve's eyes twinkled as he went on, "Rolf just beckoned to one of his followers, a big fair-haired Northman, to come and do it for him. And the big Northman stepped up to King Charles and seized his foot with such a jerk that Charles tumbled over backward and that was an end to the ceremony. The French folk were afraid to do anything to the bold strangers, so they just picked up Charles the Simple, and Rolf and his followers went off, laughing as hard as they could, to the country Rolf was to rule and which soon came to be called Normandy.

"Rolf was a good duke," went on Herve, "and made Normandy a fairly peaceful and prosperous country. There has been plenty of quarreling and fighting since then," added the old man, "but our Duke William, who is the fifth ruler since Rolf, has got things very well under control and is all the while making Normandy more prosperous and powerful."

"But you haven't told us yet why he is going to fight the British!" said Henri.

"Oh, yes," answered Master Herve, "that is because,—let me see," said he, thinking hard,—"it is because,—Oh, I have it now! The British King, Edward, who died a while ago, had no children to inherit the kingdom, so he had promised it to our Duke William. But when King Edward died, Harold, one of the powerful British nobles, got an army together and had himself made King. So our Duke William is having ships built near the mouth of the river Dives, which flows into the sea, and is getting all his soldiers ready, and in the autumn he will sail for Britain and fight for his rights. Nearly all the Norman nobles are going with him and it will be lonesome and quiet enough when our Count Bertram and all the rest are gone!"

Here Master Herve gave a deep sigh, and just at that

moment *"Boo!"* cried a merry voice, and in danced the two little girls hand in hand.

The old gate-keeper started, and smiled in spite of himself, as Marie, taking his hand, said gaily, "Well, you needn't put on such a long face, Master Herve! I guess *we'll* still be here!" and she smiled saucily at the old man who was a great favorite with all the children about the castle.

Alan and Henri jumped up laughing, and "Wait, Marie!" called out the latter, for the girls had already scampered off again.

At this they stopped and waited till the boys came up, for all four were near the same age and great playmates. "We're going to play 'turn the trencher,' " said Blanchette. "You go get one, Alan, and be *It* to start!" she coaxed.

"All right!" said Alan good-naturedly, and he ran off to the kitchen and soon came back with the trencher. By this time little Josef and several more pages had joined the group, and Alan started the game which they played exactly as children play it now; and if you do not know how that is, ask some of them to tell you.

CHAPTER IV

BLANCHETTE AND MARIE

The next morning Alan, Henri, and the other pages helped to straighten up the hall by picking up from the floor the straw-filled mattresses on which they had slept, and while they were busy with this Lady Gisla took the little girls down to the lowest story of the keep where there was a storehouse for food. Here, with the keys hanging from her girdle, she unlocked bins and closets, giving out to the cooks supplies for the day, while Blanchette and Marie watched all she did.

As they turned to go, "Mother," said Blanchette, peering into a dark passage-way in the wall, "is anybody in the dungeon?"

"I think not now," answered Lady Gisla, as she glanced toward the passage which led to a dreadful cavern-like cell burrowed under the paving-stones of the court.

For while castle folk were always guarding against some one else attacking them, they did not forget that they themselves were quite as apt to make trouble for other people and that they might sometimes bring home prisoners from their many wars and quarrels. So they always provided a dungeon or two in which to keep them. And every one was so used to such things that even if the one at Noireat had held some wretched captive, neither the little girls nor Lady Gisla would have thought anything of it.

As they left the storehouse, "Come, children," she said, "we will go to the weaving-room now."

They followed her up the winding stair to the second story of the keep in which were their sleeping-rooms, and then up still higher to a large loft where a number of the castle women were already hard at work. Some held in their hands spindles and distaffs, little wooden rods on which they were spinning and winding linen and woolen threads; while others, seated at hand looms, were weaving the threads into cloth.

"Oh, mother," said Blanchette, as she stood in front of one of the looms from which hung a small square of linen cloth, "see, I have finished my piece, and now mayn't I begin to work it? Henri has drawn a pattern for me!"

"Yes, child," answered Lady Gisla, smiling at her eager face. "Let me see the drawing. You have done your weaving very well," she added, as she examined the bit of cloth which the little girl had spun and woven herself.

Blanchette hurried to a tall chest of drawers at one

side of the room and tugging one of them open, pulled out a piece of parchment on which Henri had drawn a little girl holding a flower in her hand. He hadn't drawn it with a lead pencil, either, for nobody had any; he had used instead a pen cut from the quill of a feather and dipped in home-made ink.

As Lady Gisla looked at it, "Yes," she said, "this will do very nicely for you to learn your stitches on, and Henri has a pretty taste in drawing." She then showed Blanchette how to fasten her square of cloth in an embroidery frame, and with a needle and some colored thread helped her to begin copying the figure of the little girl.

Meantime, Marie gave a sigh as she seated herself in front of another loom where a small piece of cloth like Blanchette's was waiting to be finished. "Oh, dear," she cried, "I wish mine was ready to begin working, too!"

"Well, Marie," said Lady Gisla gently, "you know you both began at the same time, but you have not worked quite so industriously as Blanchette. But it is almost done, and I think if you try you can easily finish it to-day."

Marie set to weaving with a will, and the little girls were the picture of industry as they bent over their work. They had on blue dresses made much like Lady Gisla's, only of course their skirts were shorter and they wore no girdles and keys. Their hair was arranged in two braids with hung over their shoulders in front. Now and then Lady Gisla looked at them with a smile as they worked so busily they forgot to talk.

All cloth was then woven by hand, and every little girl, even in the castles, was early taught how to spin and weave; and, later on, those of gentle birth learned to embroider. The cloth they wove was needed not only for clothing, but also to hang on the walls of the great stone castles in which so many Normans lived. These castles were very cold in winter; and the woolen tapestries, as they were called, made the lofty halls and sleeping rooms far more comfortable than they would otherwise have been. Lady Gisla was finishing an especially handsome piece; she had woven it herself and on it she was working a hunting scene showing a forest where men on horseback and shaggy dogs were chasing a stag with branching antlers.

Presently, there was a knock on the heavy oaken door and a page entered the room. Bending on one knee before Lady Gisla, he said: "My lady, Mother Margot is in the courtyard with a basket of herbs which she says you asked her to bring."

"Why, yes," answered Lady Gisla, "they are medicine herbs. Bid her come in, and bring her here to the weaving-room."

As the page hastened off, "come, girls," she said, "you may leave your work for awhile, and we will see what Mother Margot has brought."

In a few minutes the page again opened the door and ushered in an old woman who made a courtesy as she entered. She wore a black homespun dress and a white kerchief crossed over her shoulders, and on her head a white cap with a wide fluted border. Over her arm hung a coarse basket made of osiers and in this were a number of bunches of green plants and leaves.

"Good day, Mother Margot," said Lady Gisla kindly. "Have you brought the herbs I wanted?"

"Yes, my lady," answered the old woman, who was one of the peasant folk belonging on Count Bertram's estate. "Here is boneset, and camomile, and bitter-root and tansy," and as she took the green bunches from her basket and laid them on a heavy oaken table nearby, she muttered over the names of each.

Blanchette and Marie had stood by watching with interest as Mother Margot emptied her load, and when she was gone they fell to examining the little bunches of green. "Oh," said Marie, as she took up one cluster "what pretty leaves these are! Though the medicine they'll make will probably taste nasty enough!" And she made a wry face.

"Yes," said Blanchette, laughing, "and here are some whole plants, roots and all! And likely they are worse still!"

"Those leaves you think so pretty, Marie, are from the fever-few herb," said lady Gisla, "and are very good to make medicine for persons ill of fever. And those whole plants, Blanchette, are rosemary and elecampane, and it is the roots that are the best part."

So taking up the herbs one by one, Lady Gisla explained their uses in curing illness and how they must be prepared. Some were to be dried, some boiled and the juice carefully kept, while of still others the leaves and roots must be pounded fine and steeped in various ways.

Blanchette and Marie listened attentively, for they knew that when they grew up they would be expected to know how to attend their families or friends if they fell ill. Doctors were few then and their knowledge of medicine small at best. So most people, and especially those living in the castles perched on lonely crags, had to do the best they could for themselves; and the girls of the family must learn how to prepare and use the healing herbs in the fields and forests about them, and also how to bandage wounds and care for those hurt in battle; for the men did a great deal of fighting about one thing and another.

Lady Gisla was very skillful in all these things and

had already taught the little girls a great deal. She now showed them how to sort and arrange the herbs, and it kept them busy till dinner-time.

After dinner, "Lads," said Count Bertram to Alan and Henri, "you, and the rest of the pages, get out your ponies, and Hugh and I will give you a riding-lesson."

"Yes, sir count!" answered the boys delightedly, and "Oh father," cried Blanchette, "mayn't Marie and I go, too?"

"Yes, child," said Count Bertram, "if your mother is willing."

"The children have been working all morning," said Lady Gisla, "and I think a ride will do them good. And then, of course, they must learn to be good riders as well as the boys."

"To be sure!" answered the count. "Run along, girls, and get your capes and bonnets and the boys will bring your ponies."

Presently the merry little party clattered out over the drawbridge and down the winding path to the fields. Count Bertram kept his eye on the girls, giving them many directions how to become graceful and fearless riders. Hugh attended to the pages, who must learn not only to ride with ease and fearlessness, but also to spring to their saddles without touching the stirrups and to jump their ponies over streams and walls. They must learn other outdoor things as well; how to run and leap and swim and shoot with bow and arrow, and all kinds of exercises to make them strong and manly.

When the riding lesson was over and they cantered back to Noireat, "See!" said Marie, looking up the steep bridle path, "I believe that is a minstrel going to the castle!"

"It surely is!" said Blanchette, gazing with Marie at the man climbing on foot the path ahead of them. He wore a dark tunic and a curiously fringed mantle of flame color; on his head was a gay cap and feather, and on one leg his hose was sky-blue and the other deep green. Over his shoulder, hanging by a ribbon, was a musical instrument with a few strings and shaped much like a harp.

"Goody!" cried Marie. "We will have some music this evening!"

At this Alan turned to Henri, for the two were riding just behind the little girls, and "Well, Henri," he said banteringly, "that's a good thing for you."

"Why?" asked Henri.

"Because," said Alan, "I was going to beat you this evening at that draw game of checkers we were to play!"

"I guess no!" retorted Henri. "Anyway, if you did, I can beat you any day at backgammon!" And the two boys fell to discussing their favorite games and kept it up till they found themselves once more in the castle courtyard. Here the minstrel, as the wandering poets and singers of the time were called, had already been welcomed; for the songs of the minstrels were among the favorite entertainments of the time.

After supper it was chilly, and the fire of logs was lighted in the fireplace, and though the smoke curled out into the hall and hung through the air in dim wreaths, nobody minded it when the minstrel stood up and striking the strings of his harp sang song after song, most of them telling some brave story of war or adventure.

Everyone listened with rapt attention, and clapped their hands when he finished. And no wonder people liked to have minstrels come, for the only way they knew about stories was for some one to sing or tell them to them. There were no printed books then; all were carefully written by hand, usually by the monks in the monasteries who often painted and decorated the pages in the most beautiful way, and these books were too few and precious for most people to have. Then they were not stories, anyway, but mostly religious books.

"Mother," whispered Blanchette, as she listened to the minstrel, "do you suppose I can ever learn to play like that?"

"I don't know, dear," answered Lady Gisla, who had taught the children to play a little on musical instruments at the castle. "Perhaps he will stay here a while and give you some lessons."

But when Count Bertram asked him to do so, the minstrel thanked him and "Nay, sir count," he answered, "not now. This is bluebird weather, and I am on the wing!"

He as much as said, though, that when winter came he would like to come back to Noireat. For while the minstrels preferred to wander around through the summer, they were glad enough to find some castle in which they might spend the winter time. And welcome they were, for with their songs they helped pass many a long cold evening; also they could teach such music as they knew to the girls and boys of the castle.

CHAPTER V

"The Mystery of the Rivers"

As Alan and Henri stood on either side of Count Bertram, ready to wait upon him as he was eating his breakfast, "Lad," he said, "isn't this the day for your lessons with Father Herluin?"

"Yes, sir count," answered Alan, as both boys drew a long face at the prospect.

"Never mind!" said Count Bertram, laughing good-humoredly. "Pay attention and learn what he tells you, and when you are through come to the falcon mew and I will give you a lesson more to your liking."

The boys' faces brightened at this, and when the count had finished they joined the other children and trooped off quite briskly to school in the little chapel which was part of the castle and of which Father Herluin was priest. Noble families had to provide religious services in their own homes as they generally lived too far away from any church; and the good priest was also, two or three times a week, school-master to the castle children.

When his pupils had seated themselves in the chapel,

Father Herluin first gave them a lesson on church matters. Then, taking from a shelf the written and painted prayer-book, which was the castle library, he taught them a little reading. Next came a little less arithmetic and still less of geography; this last studied from a ridiculous map made by hand and showing a very queer world with the strange animals and monsters which map-makers then put in whenever they were in doubt about places. And they were in doubt about many, for everybody thought the earth flat instead of round, and had very little idea of the true shapes of lands and seas.

Sometimes the children learned a trifle about the stars or plants or whatever else Father Herluin happened to know; but it was not much like the lessons boys and girls must learn now.

After two hours the school was over for the day; and as there were no school-books nor paper nor pencils, of course there was no studying between times.

Blanchette and Marie went back to learn some household matters from Lady Gisla, and the boys raced off to the falcon mew.

Falcons were used in hunting; and however little a boy of that time could read or write, one thing he was taught thoroughly, and that was to be an accomplished huntsman, as this was the favorite sport of those of gentle birth.

There were two kinds of hunting; that called "the mystery of the woods" consisted in chasing wild animals, such as deer or boars, through the forest; and this was much like the sport of to-day except that no one had guns then and when the dogs had finally run the poor animal to earth it was usually killed by the master of the hunt, who carried a spear or knife for the purpose.

But "mystery of the rivers," was quite a different affair as it was the chasing of birds through the sky; and, for this, falcons, very strong and swift-winged birds of the hawk family, were especially trained.

This kind of hunting was called "the mystery of the rivers" because the herons and other birds which the falcons were taught to attack made their nests on the banks of rivers. Every noble youth must know how to train and care for the falcons, and as he must learn also dozens of special works to use in speaking of the birds and their every movement it took really quite a long time to master the art of falconry, or hawking, as it was often called.

"Well, lads," said Count Bertram, who was already in the mew,—the room where the falcons were kept,—"I hope you are a great deal wiser than when I saw you last!"

"Yes, sir count," said Henri, "we learned ever so much this morning." And then he quickly added, "Have you seen my falcon, sir" I am afraid she is not well, she seems so mopy."

"Which is yours, Henri?" asked Count Bertram, looking at the dozen or more hawklike birds perched about the room. "Oh, that one over there with her head down?" he added. "I don't think there is anything the matter with her. Just try her with the lure."

Henri took a silver whistle from a shelf nearby and fastened a bit of meat to it beneath a bunch of gay feathers dangling from one end. "Wait a minute," said the count, "till Alan loosens her jesses!" And Alan hastened to unfasten from the perch the little leather thongs attached to her legs.

Henri then blew the whistle and the bird, raising its head, immediately spread its wings and in an instant had lighted on his wrist and was trying to get the bit of meat, while all the other falcons strained at their jesses and tried to reach him, too.

The whistle, or lure, was thus made attractive with feathers and meat while the birds were being trained to come when they heard it blown; for it was by the lure that the huntsman drew the falcon back to him when a hunt was over.

As Henri's bird flew toward him there was a pretty tinkling sound; and, indeed, every time any of the falcons moved about on their perches there was a musical sound, for every one of them had a tiny bell, like a little sleigh-bell, strapped around each of his legs just above the toes; and these bells and the leather jesses they always wore. Several of them wore another very odd thing, a little hood made of cloth or leather and covering the whole head, beak, eyes, and all. These hoods were put on the fiercer birds to make them tamer and protect their trainer from their beaks; also, when they were taken out to hunt all wore hoods so that nothing might distract their attention till time to begin the chase, when the head covering was plucked off.

"Whose bird is that with the red hood?" asked Count Bertram, as he noticed one of the smaller and younger birds restlessly moving on its perch and trying to shake off its gay head covering.

"Oh, that is Marie's, sir count," answered Alan, "she is very proud of that hood, and Blanchette is making a green one for hers!"

For the girls, too, had their pet falcons, and ladies often followed the sport with the men.

"Well, lads," again asked the count, "do you know your lesson in the falconry language: What do I mean when I say the falcon's 'arms'?"

"His legs, sir" answered Henri.

"And his 'sails'?" continued the count.

"His wings, sir," said Alan.

"What are his 'beams'?" again asked the count, "and what is he doing when he 'mantles,' or 'jouks,' or 'bates'?"

"His 'beams,' " answered the boys in chorus, "are the long feathers of his wings, and he 'mantles' when he stretches back one wing, when he sleeps he 'jouks,' and when he flutters to escape we must say he 'bates.'"

"Very good," said the count, smiling; and then after questioning the lads a little further, he said: "Now you may feed the birds; but don't give them much, as we will fly some of them this afternoon and they must still be hungry enough to be interested in the quarry." For so was called the bird or hare or whatever prey the falcon went in chase of.

Alan at once went to the castle kitchen where he got some pieces of beef and mutton which he placed on a bunch of feathers from the breast of a heron, one of the birds the falcons were taught to pursue. When all was ready Henri and the other pages began to shout at the tops of their voices, and going into the courtyard called about them a number of the count's hunting dogs, which they soon had yelping and bow-wowing at the tops of their voices also. This was done so the falcons might become so used to it that when they were taken out to hunt they would attack a real heron and not be disturbed or frightened by the shouting and barking that was sure to go on around them.

The count looked on approvingly, and after a few more directions, he said, "After dinner I am going out with Hugh and one or two of my squires for a little sport, and you boys may come along."

The lads' eyes danced, and just as soon as dinner was over they hurried back to the mew to bring the count his bird.

As the little party rode out the castle gate on Count Bertram's right fist perched the falcon, the jesses on its legs caught in a small hook in the back of his heavy glove and a brown hood over its head. Hugh and one of the other squires carried falcons, also, but Alan and Henri being only pages must content themselves with watching the others and learning all they could.

They rode down the cliff road and through the meadows till they came to a little river, fringed by willow and poplar trees.

Presently, "Look!" cried Alan to Henri, in a low voice, as up from a cluster of willows a blue heron rose in flight.

At the same moment Count Bertram, who was riding in front, quickly plucking the hood from his falcon's head, with a shrill cry, "Haw! Haw! Ho now!" loosed it for pursuit. "Haw! Haw! Ho now!" shouted Hugh and the other squires; for this was one of the cries by which the falcons were taught to speed to the attack.

But Count Bertram's bird needed no urging as up, up it soared, mounting the air in great spiral curves.

Meantime, the poor heron, seeing its pursuer, was trying its best to fly away.

As the little party of huntsmen dashed along breathlessly watching the two birds, up, up, still higher soared the falcon, till for an instant it poised, a dark speck in the blue sky, while beneath it the blue heron fled on frightened wings. Then, like lightening, the falcon swooped down, hurling its powerful body full upon the heron, striking it with such force that it dropped to earth stunned by the blow. In another moment the falcon was upon it, and the jingle of little bells told only too plainly how claws and beak were doing their deadly work.

"Bravo!" cried Count Bertram. "What think you, Hugh? Was not that a pretty flight?"

"Yes, sir count," answered Hugh with enthusiasm, "the falcon went like an arrow to the mark!"

After Count Bertram had flown his bird a few more times the two squires took turns with theirs. Later on, as the afternoon waned, each of the huntsmen took the little silver lure, which dangled from his wrist, and whistled his falcon back, and the three birds were again hooded and each fastened securely to the glove of his master.

When the party returned to the castle, Count Bertram handed his falcon to Alan to be placed in the mew; and as the boy carefully received it the count looked critically to see that he held his elbow crooked at just the right angle, and that his fist was doubled up in precisely the correct way to carry the bird; for all these matters were considered as important to be learned as any lesson in manners.

THE BOYS…TOOK A FENCING LESSON FROM HUGH.

CHAPTER VI

LITTLE DUKE RICHARD

All morning a fine rain had fallen and the boys and girls of the castle had been busy indoors; the girls learning to sew and embroider, while the boys, with blunt swords, took a fencing lesson from Hugh.

After dinner Blanchette peeped out into the courtyard. "It's still raining!" she called back to Marie and the pages who were gathered around the door. "What shall we do?"

"Let's go over to Master Herve and get him to tell us a story!" proposed Marie.

"All right!" cried the others, and darting out of the door, they skimmed like a flight of swallows over the wet paving stones to old Herve's tower. As the laughing group burst into the place, "Well, well!" he exclaimed in pretended fright, "I thought the Duke himself was storming the castle, you made such a hub-bub!"

"We will storm your tower, sure enough, Master Herve," cried Marie, "unless you tell us a nice story right away!"

"Dear me," answered Master Herve, "if that is so, I

will hurry and begin! What shall I tell you? About little Duke Richard?"

"Yes," shouted a chorus of merry voices, "tell us about little Duke Richard!"

"Well," began Master Herve, "it was a long time ago"—"*How* long?" asked Henri, who always liked to be exact,—"Oh, I don't know," replied Master Herve, "but it must have been a good while, because it was when Richard was a little boy only eight years old, and Richard was the great-great-grandfather of our Duke William, so you see it must have been nearly ninety years ago.

"There was a great deal of quarreling in Normandy then, and Duke William Long-Sword—"

"Who was Duke William Long-Sword?" asked one of the younger pages.

"Why, he was little Richard's father," put in Alan, "and he was called Long-Sword because he always carried a wonderful long one with a gold handle!"

"Yes," said old Herve, "you are right, Alan, he was Richard's father, and as I began to say, when the little lad was only eight years old William Long-Sword was one day killed by some of his enemies."

"Tell about his hair shirt!" said Henri; for the children had heard most of old Herve's stories before, and did not want anything left out.

"To be sure!" answered Herve. "When they came to make Duke William ready for his funeral, they found that underneath his splendid ducal dress he always wore a shirt made of coarse hair cloth next to his skin, and that he kept a little scourge with which he often whipped himself. For he was very pious, and you know that is the way that many people believe they can make peace with God for their sins."

Here the children made long faces at the idea of any one whipping himself, and Master Herve went on: "The funeral was no sooner over than little Richard, who was the sole heir to the duchy, was dressed in his handsomest red tunic and brought to the cathedral in the city of Rouen to be crowned Duke of Normandy.

"Richard walked up the aisle, and when he sat in the great chair by the altar his feet didn't come anywhere near the floor. The priest said the mass, and Richard solemnly promised to be a good and true ruler; and then they put on his shoulders the great crimson velvet mantle trimmed with ermine that belongs to the Norman dukes. But Richard was so little that it trailed all around him, and when they tried to crown him the crown was so big and heavy that one of the barons had to hold it over his head. Then they gave him the long sword that had been his father's. When it was over, and Richard stood up to walk down the aisle, the mantle was so long and heavy that one of the nobles picked him up and carried him; another was about to take the sword."

"But Richard wouldn't let him! He carried it himself!" cried Henri.

"Yes," said old Herve, "thought the sword was longer than he was, he would let no one take it."

"It must have been a funny sight," observed Marie, "to see him carried down the long aisle with that big crimson mantle trailing behind him and he clutching the sword taller than himself!"

The others laughed, but Master Herve did not join them, "Yes, funny it may seem to you youngsters, but it was a sad enough sight to the friends of little Richard to see him orphaned and obliged to be a duke before he was able to govern the country, and with all sorts of troublesome affairs ahead of him and, worst of all, the King of France wishing with all his heart to get his duchy from him!

"Well, Richard was carried back to the palace, and then his vassals, the highest nobles of Normandy, all came and kneeling before him, placed their great strong hands between his baby ones and swore to be loyal subjects."

"Didn't Richard himself have to do the same thing to the King of France?" asked Alan.

"Yes," said old Herve, "he did later on, the first time he went to France, and he didn't go of his own free will, either; but that's what I'm coming to in the story. Of course ever since Rolf the Ganger promised loyalty to Charles the Simple all the Norman dukes have done the same to the kings of France. But though the French people have kept fairly peaceable with us, they have never liked it because Rolf took Normandy, and our dukes have known well enough that behind their backs they called them 'Dukes of the Pirates,' for so the French nick-named our brave people. And no sooner was little Richard crowned than the French King Louis thought it would be a fine thing to get possession of the young Duke of the Pirates, and then—well, King Louis had two boys of his own, and of course if anything happened to Richard that crimson velvet mantle and the big crown would do very nicely for one of the little French princes." Here old Herve shrugged his shoulders with a wise look.

"At any rate," he went on, "very soon King Louis came and insisted on taking Richard home with him. He said the boy was his godson, and his vassal besides, and that he had a perfect right to be his guardian. The Norman nobleman thought very differently, but as the King had taken care to bring a large force of soldiers with him they did not dare to refuse. Though when they said good-by to their little duke they made up their minds to get him back again just as soon as they could manage it. One of their number, a young noble, was allowed to go with him, and a faithful friend he proved. Who of you remembers his name?" quizzed the old man of his eager little listeners.

"We *all* do! Osmond de Centeville!" cried the children in chorus, indignant that Master Herve should fancy they could forget.

"It was a sad journey for poor little Richard," he continued, "away from his own home to the gloomy castle of Laon where King Louis was then living; and when they reached it Richard found nothing but coldness and unkindness from all. The Queen, Gerberge, was haughty and disagreeable, and the two young princes, Pothaire and Carloman, were cross and hateful to him.

"Several months went on in this way; but all the while Richard's faithful friend, Osmond de Centeville, was keeping careful watch for the very first chance to help his little master to escape.

"By and by, Richard fell ill; and the paler and thinner he grew the happier it made king Louis and Queen Gerberge, who wanted him to die so as to get Normandy for their hateful young Lothaire."

Here Alan and Henri clenched their fists angrily, as if

they could have liked to get at Richard's cruel enemies, while Blanchette sighed sympathetically, and Marie, remembering their lesson on herbs, asked: "Didn't Osmond know any place where he could get some herb medicine? I should think he could have managed *some* way!"

"Don't you fancy Osmond de Centeville wasn't taking the best care of Richard!" said old Herve with a chuckle. "I dare say he got plenty of medicine for him, and gave it to him himself up there in the tower room where he kept him away from the castle folks. And he went right down into the castle kitchen, too, and cooked everything that Richard ate, because he was afraid the King's cooks had been ordered to poison little Richard! Well, one night everybody was so sure that the Duke of the Pirates was going to die, that they thought there was no need of keeping as close watch on him as they had been doing, and King Louis and Queen Gerberge decided to give a great banquet because they were so happy at the idea of soon getting Normandy for Lothaire.

"So, while everybody was busy eating, Osmond managed to get a big armful of straw from somewhere, and with this he crept quietly up the winding stair to the tower room where Richard was lying very white and weak.

" 'Hush!' he whispered, as the little duke started up in surprise. 'Can you keep as still as a mouse for a little while, and not mind if you are nearly smothered? And can you pretend that you are not a duke at all, but nothing but a bundle of straw?'

" 'Yes, yes!!' answered Richard eagerly, his eyes growing bright with excitement as Osmond explained his plan, 'I can be a stick of wood, *anything*, Osmond, if you will only take me away from here!'

"Then Osmond rolled Richard up in his little purple mantle and stuffed him into the middle of that bundle of straw, and, seizing it in his strong arms, he crept out of the room, and felt his way carefully down the winding stairs, till presently he came to the big smoky kitchen which he had to pass through in order to get out doors. The cooks were all so busy running to and from that very few of them noticed Osmond at all, and those who did were quite satisfied when he said, with a fine careless air, 'I forgot to bed down and feed my war horse and I'm just going out to the stable to do it.'

"And Osmond went to the stable, sure enough," went on Master Herve with a laugh, but it was neither to make a bed out of the little duke nor to feed him to the big Normandy horse which he saddled and bridled faster than he had ever done in all his life. Then, placing the precious bundle of straw across the saddle bow, carefully,—oh, so carefully,—he led the horse to the castle gate. The keeper had had so much wine at the banquet that his head had dropped on his breast and he was sound asleep. And carefully,—oh, so carefully,—Osmond slipped back the great bars, one by one, flung open the gate, sprang into the saddle, and away with the wind!"

Here there was a loud clapping of hands and a shrill cheer from Herve's little audience.

"Oh," cried Henri enviously, "wouldn't I like to have been Osmond!"

"Maybe you would," said old Herve, "but I don't believe anybody would like to have been the Duke of the Pirates that night, for the poor little fellow was nearly smothered! When Osmond had galloped a safe distance from the castle, he stopped and loosened the straw as much as he could from around Richard's face, for the little lad was fairly gasping. But he was full of pluck and without fear,—you know the name he earned in after life?" asked Herve, who was fond of quizzing children.

"Yes," they answered, "of course we do, 'Richard the Fearless'!"

"So," went on Herve, "after a short rest, on they galloped fast and faster, clatter, clatter, clatter, every minute drawing nearer the Norman border. Oh, but that was a wild ride that brought the little Duke of the Pirates back to his own! All night they rode, and far into the next day till the good black war horse was spent and breathless. Then Osmond somehow managed to get a fresh one, and thud, thud, away they went again. At daybreak the second day they came to the river Epte dividing France and Normandy, and on the cliffs at the far side rose the towers of Crecy castle. There was no bridge, but that was no matter. Panting and foam-flecked, straight into the river plunged the gallant horse with his precious bundle. Oh, how tired he was with that long galloping, but how bravely he fought his way across the current and safe to the farther side! And then, just as he had won back to his own Normandy, it seemed for a moment that all was lost for the little duke. For the watchers of the castle walls, little dreaming who were the riders of that brave horse, and thinking them enemies from France, were just fitting their arrows to their bows to shoot, when at a quick signal from Osmond they paused, and then,—well, when they found out that their own true duke was come back to them, you can guess whether or not they gave his a rousing welcome!" and old Herve's voice rose in enthusiastic fervor.

"But with all his bravery," added Herve, in a tender tone, "the poor little man was scarce breathing when they lifted him out of his straw and loosened his purple mantle; for the long ride had almost ended his life. But you can guess, too, whether they nursed him carefully. And you may be sure the lady of Crecy castle saw that he got the right herb medicine"; here Master Herve looked at Marie with a twinkle in his eye. "At any rate, it wasn't long till the little duke was as fine and sturdy a boy as heart could wish and King Louis didn't get him back again, either!"

"No," said Alan, "when he came back and tried to, the Norman army was waiting for him, and he decided he would have to look somewhere else for a duchy for Lothaire!"

"Yes, yes, youngsters," said old Herve, "I guess you know all my stories nearly as well as I do. But I am tired now, so go off and play. Next time you come maybe I'll have a new story for you."

CHAPTER VII

The Tournament

It was the day of the tournament and every one in the castle was up at dawn. Breakfast was soon over, and then, while the rest were getting ready, Hugh brought Count Bertram his armor and helped him to put it on. First came the hauberk, a tunic of leather over which were sewed hundreds of small iron rings, so close together that a spear point could not pierce them. Hugh slipped this over the count's shoulders and then on his head he placed the helmet: a close-fitting pointed cap also of leather sewn with iron rings.

Though the helmet did not entirely cover Count Bertram's face, it came over his ears and laced under his chin and a stiff piece of leather hung down over his forehead and nose, giving him such as odd look that Hugh smiled as he fastened it on.

"Are my lance and shield ready?" asked Count Bertram.

"Yes, sir count," answered Hugh. "There they are," and he pointed to a long lance leaning against the wall and close by it a large kite-shaped shield of wood on which was painted a red two-legged dragon.

Here the little page, Josef, came running in, and making a stiff bow he sank on one knee and bashfully holding out a scarlet embroidered ribbon, he said, "Sir Count Bertram, here is the—the—the *token* Lady Gisla made for you!"

"Good!" said Count Bertram, smiling, "that was a hard word to remember, wasn't it, Josef?" And the little lad blushed and nodded his head as Hugh, taking the ribbon, tied it in one of the rings on Count Bertram's helmet.

For at tournaments each knight usually wore some token given him by his lady love. Often it was a ribbon, a glove or a flower, and if he won the prize the knight always declared that he had striven for it in honor of his lady.

By the time Count Bertram was ready so were all the rest; and Lady Gisla herself came into the hall looking lovely in a green gown embroidered in silver. She wore a jewelled girdle and necklace and on her head a wonderful tall cap from the back of which floated a veil of fine lace. Blanchette and Marie, who were to go along, fairly danced with excitement as they put on their frocks of blue silk and little caps and riding capes of scarlet cloth.

"Oh, mother, aren't we ready to start?" cried Blanchette, running to the door of the great hall.

"Alan! Alan!" called Marie impatiently. "Where are our ponies?"

"Do not be in such a hurry, children," said Lady Gisla, "we will soon be off. The pages and squires are putting the trappings on the horses now; for you know they must be dressed in their best, just as we are."

"Oh, how fine they look!" exclaimed Marie, as she and Blanchette ran down to the courtyard.

The horses, indeed, looked very gay, with saddles and bridles of richly worked leather and bright colored rosettes and tassels dangling from their ears and the various straps about their bodies. Over the saddles for the ladies of the party were flung pieces of scarlet cloth embroidered in colors.

Presently all was ready and off they started. And what a merry ride it was, the five miles to the castle of Brecey! By and by, across a field of red poppies, they saw tall towers rising from a steep hill.

"See!" cried Blanchette to Alan who was next to her, "that must be Brecey castle, for silk banners are on the tower!"

"Yes," said Alan, "but I do not believe we will go up

there yet. You know the herald said the tournament would be held in the meadow near by.”

Just then as they rounded another bend in the road, “Oh,” said Marie, “there is the place now!” And, sure enough, they could see the meadow where a large number of gayly dressed people had already gathered.

On reaching the place, Count Bertram and his party were warmly welcomed by the lord and lady of Brecey, who at once sent a page to conduct Lady Gisla and her attendants to the raised wooden seats that had been built at one side of the meadow. In the middle of these was a throne-like chair covered with bright tapestry, and there sat a beautiful lady richly dressed and wearing a wreath of flowers in her hair.

Blanchette and Marie, who had clung shyly to Lady Gisla as they followed the page, now gazed at the lady in rapt admiration. “Oh, mother,” whispered Blanchette, “is she a queen?”

“Yes, dear,” said Lady Gisla with a smile, “not a real queen, but the Queen of the Tournament, and she will give the prize to the winner.”

When they took their places on the seats a number of ladies were all around them, and bright banners fluttered everywhere.

“See, children,” said Lady Gisla, pointing to a large

oval space in front of the seats and in-closed by a double railing of wood, "that is called the 'lists,' and is where the knights will fight one another. The squires and pages will stand outside, between the railings, so that if any one in the lists is hurt or needs anything they will be ready to help."

"Oh, Lady Gisla!" cried Marie, whose bright eyes had been eagerly searching the groups of horsemen gathered behind a rope at each end of the lists. "There is Count Bertram at the far end!"

"Yes!" cried Blanchette. "And Alan and Henri are fixing his spurs and doing something to his saddle!"

"They are probable seeing that none of the straps have become unfastened," said Lady Gisla, watching with interest as all was being made ready.

In a little while a herald rode around the lists blowing short sharp blasts on a trumpet. When everybody pricked up their ears to listen, he stood up in his stirrups and in a loud voice called out the rules of the tournament and what the prizes were to be.

"What does he mean by saying the lances of the knights must all have 'coronals' on them?" asked Blanchette.

"I am not quite sure," answered Lady Gisla, for tournaments and their rules were still rather too new in Normandy to be very well known, "but I think coronals are

BLOWING SHORT, SHARP BLASTS ON A TRUMPET.

the pieces of wood that are put on the tips of the lances to blunt them so the fight will not be so dangerous." And Lady Gisla sighed, for sports in those days were very rough and in the mock fights people were often as badly hurt as in real ones.

But here a shout went up at either end of the lists as, at a signal from the Baron of Brecey, the ropes were drawn aside and the knights, spurring their horses, rushed at each other with levelled lances and the tournament began.

Blanchette and Marie, each with a long "Oh!" leaned forward in breathless interest, and Lady Gisla, with anxious gaze, fixed her eyes on Count Bertram, who was trying to overthrow a tall knight from whose helmet dangled the embroidered glove of his lady.

"Oh, hear!" cried Blanchette, "See, he has almost pushed father from his saddle!"

But in another moment Count Betram, dextrously turning his horse, by a powerful thrust of his lance sent the tall knight tumbling to the ground; and instantly his squires and pages rushed into the lists and bore off their master to a place of safety. For by this time there was a general prancing of horses and clashing of lances as each knight was trying to overthrow some one else.

Before long more than one had been borne from the field severely hurt; for in spite of the coronals on the lances there were plenty of ways to get hard knocks in a tournament, especially those earlier ones. But then, people expected such things, and no one except their nearest friends paid much attention to the wounded.

Through it all Lady Gisla and the little girls had been watching Count Bertram with eager interest; and though sometimes in the thick of the struggle they lost sight of him, when the herald blew the trumpet, which was the signal to stop fighting, to their great delight they saw that he still sat his horse erect and unharmed. And what was their pride and joy to hear the herald, as he rode slowly around the lists, proclaim that Count Bertram, of the castle of Noireat, had won the first prize of the gilded spurs, as he had overthrown four other knights.

The other ladies seated around them turned envious eyes on Lady Gisla, who was smiling her pleasure, while Blanchette and Marie were clapping their hands with delight.

"Watch, children," said Lady Gisla, "and see the Queen of the Tournament bestow the prize.

Again the little girls bent forward eagerly and looked as Count Bertram, slowly riding past the benches on which the ladies were seated, paused in front of the throne of the queen. Alan and Henri, who were walking on either side of him, at once took his bridle and helped him dismount. Then, bowing low, he knelt before the Queen of the Tournament, as, placing the spurs in his hands, she said, "Count Bertram, I bestow this prize upon you, and may you live long and happily and always do honor to your lady!"

Count Bertram, after thanking her with all knightly courtesy, rose to his feet, and the winner of the second prize took his place before the queen.

The next thing, the Baron of Brecey invited the company to make their way across the meadow and up the narrow path to his castle where a great feast was spread.

After the feast some musicians came in and played on curious old stringed instruments while the grown people danced; the boys and girls, who were not expected to join, gathered in little groups at the sides of the hall and looked on.

Late in the afternoon the party from Noireat took their leave, Count Bertram wearing his new golden spurs, and everybody in the little procession fairly bursting with pride because he had won them.

CHAPTER VIII

OLD HERVE TELLS ANOTHER STORY

Though the tournament had been several days before, the children were still talking about it to Master Herve. At last, when they had all told everything they could remember, Henri said to the old man, "Now, Master Herve, you must tell *us* a story; it's your turn!"

"Well, well," said old Herve, "what shall it be?"

"Tell us something about Duke William!" exclaimed Marie. "You have told us about other dukes, but I would like to know something more about him."

"Our Duke William is a wonderful man," said Herve, "but great and strong and powerful as he is now, I can remember the time, forty years ago, when he was just a tiny baby, and folks said that when he first reached out his little hand he clutched hold of a straw from the floor where he lay and held it so tightly that the wise women who saw him declared it was a sign he would hold fast in after life to whatever dominion he might win.

"But it didn't look much then, nor for a long while after, as if he would ever have much dominion to hold."

"Why not?" asked Blanchette.

"Because none of the Norman nobles were his friends. They all hated the helpless baby; for though his father was the Duke Robert the Magnificent, and the true descendant of Rolf the Ganger, his mother was not noble but the daughter of a tanner of leather which, you know, is a grade looked down on in Normandy. She was a very beautiful girl, and Duke Robert had first seen her one day when she was washing clothes in the little stream that flows near the castle of Falaise where he was then living."

"Why was he called 'the Magnificent'?" asked Alan.

"Well," said Herve, "that was because he was very rich and spent a great deal of money, though often he spent it very foolishly. He was very fond of little William, and proud of his handsome face and bright ways. But when William was only seven years old Duke Robert made up his mind to go on a pilgrimage."

"Why do people go on pilgrimages, Master Herve?" interrupted one of the pages.

"They go because they want to pray at some holy place to have their sins forgiven," answered Herve.

"Did you ever go?" asked another of the children.

"No," replied Master Herve, "but my father did once. He went to Saint Michael's Mount, a very holy island near Normandy. It was when I was a little chap not half so big as Josef there," and Herve nodded to little Josef sitting between Blanchette and Marie. "It was the year 1000, and for some reason or another folks got it into their heads that the world was coming to an end. So they thought a good deal about their sins and the next world, and all who could started off on pilgrimages."

"Did the world come to an end?" asked little Josef, with wide eyes.

"No, no child!" laughed Master Herve. "This is the same old world that it was sixty-six years ago. Nothing happened, but people had got so in the habit of making pilgrimages that pilgrims have been plenty ever since. And many of them are noble, too, like Duke Robert the Magnificent."

"Did he walk all the way?" inquired Blanchette. "And did he carry a staff and wear a brown robe and a broad-brimmed hat and a rope around his waist, like the pilgrims who come here so often to eat and stay all night?"

"Do you suppose he wore a hair shirt, Master Herve, like Duke William Long-Sword?" asked Henri.

"Indeed he *didn't,*" replied old Herve with another laugh; "Duke Robert wasn't that kind! He put on his best clothes and went off on horseback and took along quantities of good things to eat and ever so many people to wait on him; and when he got tired riding he had six black men to carry him in a kind of fancy bed. I dare say he did get tired, though," added Herve, "for it wasn't to any of the shrines in Normandy that he went; no, Duke Robert had made up his mind to go way off to Jerusalem.

"Before he started he gathered the Norman nobles together and insisted that they promise to be loyal to little William; he wished them to consider him their overlord while he was away. The nobles were very proud and haughty, and most of them didn't at all like the idea of promising loyalty to the little boy. But at last they consented, though some of them were very angry about it and said a great many disagreeable things behind Duke Robert's back.

"Duke Robert, however, placed little William in the care of his cousin, Alan of Brittany, and then set out on his pilgrimage.

"Everything about his party was very splendid, and as he came near the Holy Land he had his horse shod with silver shoes and ordered them nailed on so loosely that every once in a while one would tumble off in the road for anybody to pick up who happened along. Of course this was a very silly thing to do, but Duke Robert seemed to like to do queer extravagant things.

"It was a long, long journey; but a last he reached Jerusalem and prayed at all the holy places, and then he started home again. But he never came back to Normandy, for he died on the way.

"The journey had taken three years, so William was ten years old when the news reached Normandy that his father was dead. He was a very friendless little boy indeed; and before long his guardian, Alan of Brittany, was murdered. Everybody was fighting everybody else and there was no safety anywhere. To be sure, things weren't quite so bad from Wednesday evenings till Monday mornings."

"Why was that?" asked one of the children.

"Why, that was because there was so much lawlessness and bloodshed that the church proclaimed what was called the 'Truce of God,' which meant that people must not rob or kill each other on certain days of the week. But between Mondays and Wednesdays," went on the old man with a sigh, "they seemed to make up for lost time. Of course there is still a good deal of quarreling and fighting here and there in Normandy, but it's nothing to what it was when Duke William was a boy!"

"What did he do?" asked Alan.

"Well, to tell the truth," answered the old man, "I don't know how in the world the lad ever managed to pull along and hold his own against all he had to contend with; but he did it somehow. I guess just because he's a born ruler. When he was fifteen he demanded to be made a knight."

"Oh, Master Herve," exclaimed Henri, "did you know Hugh is to be made a knight and go with Count Bertram to Britain?"

"Yes," said Herve, "Hugh will be twenty-one and has served his time as page and squire. But Duke William was only fifteen, remember, yet a brave knight he was; and he *had* to be alert and fearless, for his enemies were all about him. One time he had a very narrow escape. He was at his castle of Valognes, and sound asleep in the middle of the night, when suddenly there came a quick knocking at his door; it was his fool, Goelet."

"His fool?" echoed one of the younger pages, inquiringly.

"Yes," said Marie, "I remember last year when the Baron of Gisors came to visit Count Bertram, how he brought along a funny little man they called his fool. He was queerly dressed, and had a cap all covered with bells like a falcon wears!"

"And it jingled all the while," broke in Blanchette, "and he carried a short stick that he called a bauble; it had a little head with donkey ears carved at one end! And he capered around and said anything he pleased to the baron, and everybody laughed at him!"

"Yes," said Herve, "many nobles and kings keep such a fool, or jester, whose business it is to amuse them. But when William's fool knocked on his door with his bauble that night, it wasn't any joke. 'Master!' he cried, 'Quick, get up! I have just heard of a plot your enemies have made against you, and they are coming now to take you!'

"William jumped out of bed, hurried on his clothes, rushed down the winding stair to the stable, jumped on the back of his horse and galloped out into the dark, off toward his strong castle of Falaise.

"All night he galloped, helter-skelter, over fields and ditches, any way that was the shortest cut to Falaise.

"Duke William never forgot that wild ride for his life; and, long after, he had the helter-skelter path he had taken made into a fine road which is called 'the Duke's Road.'

"But though William was safe for a time at Falaise, his enemies were still plotting against him; and soon his cousin, Guy of Burgundy, began to claim that he ought to be duke instead of William.

"Then William gathered together all his friends he could and got the King of France to help him. Guy of Burgundy, collected all the Normans who were enemies of William and a great battle was fought at a place called Val-es-Dunes. In the end William conquered, and after that almost all the nobles went over to his side.

"Yes, indeed, out Duke William is a wonderful man," repeated old Herve, "and the greatest ruler Normandy has ever had."

"Who will rule Normandy while he is gone to Britain?" asked Alan.

"Why," said Master Herve, "I hear it said the Duchess Matilda will. Duke William has such a high opinion of his wife, the duchess, that he is not afraid to trust Normandy to her care."

"Mother says Duchess Matilda is a wonderful woman," said Blanchette, "and that nobody can embroider so well as she can!"

"Yes," answered Herve, "she is a great lady. Duke William had a good deal of trouble to get her, but he was so in love with her that he won out in the end."

"Why did he have trouble to get her?" asked Marie.

"Well," said old Herve, "I guess she was willing enough, and so was her father the rich and powerful Count of Flanders, but it seems some people said she and William were relations and the laws of the church forbid relations to marry each other. I don't believe they are more than fourth or fifth cousins, if that; but at any rate some of William's enemies told a different story to the Pope, the head of the church, so for four years the lovers were kept apart. Then one day Duke William hurried up to his castle of Eu, on the border of Flanders and Normandy, met the Lady Matilda, and they were quickly married by a parish priest and then came to William's palace in the city of Rouen. And if they had no splendid processions at their wedding they had plenty afterward, for all the way to Rouen the people cheered them and gave great parties for them and greeted them right royally. And everybody said there wasn't a handsomer couple in all Normandy.

"The Pope was greatly displeased about it, but at last he forgave them, only making each promise to build a church as penance for getting married without his permission."

"And did they build them?" asked Blanchette.

"Yes, indeed, child!" answered Herve. "Duke William and Duchess Matilda always keep their word. They began the churches right away in the city of Caen, and they are so fine and grand that it has taken these twenty years since to finish them. They built them right willingly though, for all Normandy knows that the duke and duchess love each other and their marriage is very happy.

"But run along now, children! I have told you enough for one day!"

CHAPTER IX
Hugh Becomes a Knight

The summer was wearing away and the time drawing near for Count Bertram to go to Dives to join the expedition against Britain.

Meantime Hugh had reached his twenty-first birthday and was soon to become a knight. He had served faithfully his seven years as page and seven more as squire, a long and careful training; and the final ceremony of receiving knighthood was so important that it took two days to go through it, and the lords and ladies from several neighboring castles had been invited to come and help him celebrate.

In the ceremony of knighting there was much that had a symbolic meaning; that is, that was meant to remind the youth of other and higher things. Thus, when Hugh began his preparations, first of all two of the other squires took him to a special bath; and when he put off his ordinary clothes they laid them aside, as he was supposed in like way to put off his old life and enter the new with both a clean heart and clean body.

Alan and Henri were allowed to bring his new garments to him; and as still another squire took them from the chest in the castle hall were they had been kept ready, the two lads looked at them with interest, for there were three different tunics, one white, one red, and one black.

As they watched Hugh's friends help him put on the white tunic first, "Why does he put on a white one?" asked Alan.

"That is to symbolize the whiteness and purity of the life he must lead as a knight," answered the squire. Then over the white tunic they put the red one, "This," the boys were told, "is to symbolize the red blood he must be willing to shed for Christ and the defense of the church. And the black one which goes on last of all, over the red, is to signify the mystery of death which every man must bravely face."

When Hugh was thus dressed, Father Herluin came and led him to the chapel of the castle where he must stay until the next morning. He must touch neither food nor drink, nor must he sleep when night came. He was expected to spend the hours in thinking over the new life he was about to enter, and in praying God to forgive his past sins and to give him strength to keep truly and honorably the solemn vows of knighthood which he would take the next day.

And while Hugh watched and prayed, all the others were busy preparing for the morrow when the guests were to come; of course these would bring along a number of attendants, and a great feast was to follow the knighting. The long boards for the tables were scoured and so were the wooden trenchers and pewter cups for the humbler guests, while the silver flagons and dishes for the noble folks were polished till they shone. Fresh rushes were strewn on the floor, and plenty of logs brought in for the great fireplace where the cooking would go on.

"Oh, mother," said Blanchette, "isn't your new tapestry finished so we can hang it up?"

"Not quite, dear," answered Lady Gisla, who still had a little more to do on the hunting scene she had spent so much time embroidering.

"Oh, but it is so near done and so pretty, please let us put it up for to-morrow!" begged Blanchette.

"Very well," said Lady Gisla, and she gave orders to have the tapestry hung on the wall over the dais, where it looked very handsome.

Indeed, every one worked so busily and all were so tired when night came that they slept soundly, quite forgetting the young squire who kept his lonely vigil in the chapel.

Hugh tried his best to keep awake and fix his thoughts

on higher things; but sometimes his head would nod in spite of himself, and then he would have to rouse himself with an effort and try to forget that he was hungry and thirsty, and to remember that a knight must bear all hardships unflinchingly and must never shrink from any hororable task.

At last the long night wore away and the castle folk began to wake up. Count Bertram and Lady Gisla put on their best clothes and made ready to welcome their guests, who soon began to arrive.

And while the bustle of welcome was going on in the courtyard and within the castle, at the kitchen end of the great hall the cooks were scurrying about in great haste. "Rouse up, Towser! Hurry up, Bowser!" they would cry out to the patient dogs turning the spits by the big fireplace. "Faster, faster! Don't you see that venison is burning?"

And then the poor beasts would turn back their ears and trot round and round, while the venison and woodcocks and hares and whatnot on the long spits sputtered and roasted and dripped savory juices over the glowing coals. "Quick, bring me some honey and spices for these marchpanes," called one of the cooks to a boy scullion, who ran as fast as his legs would carry him to the honey-pot and spice bags so that the sweetmeants might not be delayed. "Here! Fill this flagon with cider and bring another cheese from the store-room!" commanded another; and so the work went busily on till all was ready.

By this time all the guests had come, and the pages had begun to usher them to the chapel. Heading the procession went Count Bertram, who, on greeting Hugh at the chapel door, hung around his neck the sword which was to be his. When all were seated, Hugh walked slowly up the aisle and unbuckling the sword laid it reverently upon the altar. Then, with bowed head, he knelt at the feet of Father Herluin, while the good priest, after praying that the sword might never be drawn for an unworthy cause, blessed both it and Hugh and said the service of the church.

After this the young man was taken possession of for a few minutes by Lady Gisla nd the noble ladies, her guests, for it was their duty to put on him the armor he was to wear as a knight. First of all they buckled on his spurs; and then, as Alan and Henri handed them each piece, they arrayed him in his hauberk, girt on his sword belt and set his helmet upon his head. Last of all, taking his sword from the altar Lady Gisla placed it in the scabbard at the young man's side.

When the ladies had finished their task, Hugh knelt

before Count Bertram and solemnly promised to keep faithfully the vows of knighthood which Count Bertram repeated to him. There were a great many of these, the chief being that he must fear, reverence, and serve God religiously, that he must be a loyal defender of his native land and of its ruler, that he must uphold the rights of the weak, must be gentle and courteous to all women and succor them if in distress, and that he must always speak the truth and make any sacrifice to keep his faith and honor untarnished.

When Hugh had taken the vows, and while he still knelt, Count Bertram drew his own sword from its scabbard and with the flat of it lightly struck him three times on the shoulder, at the same time pronouncing the words "In the name of God and Saint Michael I dub thee knight!"

When Hugh rose to his feet his face beamed with joy to think that his long years of service were ended and he was at last a knight.

There was one thing more, however, that must be done to finish the ceremony. For just as he had put on the three tunics to symbolize different things, so now he must mount his war-horse to signify that he was ready to ride forth to do brave and gallant deeds.

Hugh's young friends had already decked the horse in

"IN THE NAME OF GOD AND SAINT
MICHAEL I DUB THEE KNIGHT!"

his finest trappings and led him to the chapel door, where Alan and Henri stood holding his bridle on either side.

As the company came out of the chapel the young knight mounted and rode several times around the court-yard, the horse prancing and stepping proudly and seeming to feel that he, too, had become of more importance since he was no longer to be ridden by a mere squire, but would henceforth be the war-horse of a noble knight.

When Hugh finally halted in front of the keep, and sprang to the ground, everybody crowded around him with smiles and good wishes for the new life he had entered, and then Count Bertram led the way to the castle hall and the knighting ended with a merry feast.

CHAPTER X
ON THE WAY TO DIVES

It was late in August, and on almost every road in Normandy one might have seen soldiers making their way to the sea-coast town of Dives to join the forces of Duke William for the invasion of Britain.

At the castle of Noireat all was ready for Count Bertram's going. Several days before, a number of knights, who were his vassals, had come with their followers to go with him, and the castle had been overflowing with people. At last, when the morning came to start, there was a great running to and fro; squires and pages bustled about harnessing the horses, putting on their rosettes and plumes, and then they helped their masters buckle on their armor and spurs. Count Bertram's had been freshly polished, and Lady Gisla had made for him a new banner of blue silk on which was worked a red two-legged dragon like that painted on his shield.

As the little party said good-by, "Oh, father," cried Blanchette, clinging to him with tearful eyes, "don't get hurt! Promise you will come back safe and sound!"

And Count Bertram patted her head and kissing her and Lady Gisla declared that he would come home just as soon as they had helped Duke William conquer Britain.

Then all mounted their horses, Count Bertram and Hugh and the other knights riding in front, and after them the squires, who carried such baggage as was needful, while last of all came Alan and Henri, who were to go along as far as Dives, ready always to wait upon the others or do errands at their bidding.

Master Herve, with trembling hands, opened the castle gate, and off they rode, their armor gleaming and their banners fluttering in the summer sunlight.

As the old man watched them go he shook his head sadly, and "Well, well," he muttered to himself, "old Herve has seen the day when he didn't have to stay behind and sit on his bench from morning till night! Many's the time I've followed Count Bertram's father to the field!" And he blinked his eyes hard as he shut the great gate.

As for Lady Gisla and the little girls, they climbed to the top of the very highest tower in the castle and there they watched the party of riders as they wound down the cliff and out upon the road, gazing until they could see no more.

Meantime Count Bertram and the others rode along on their way to the town of Falaise where they were to pass the night. Alan and Henri, who had never been far from home, looked about with bright eyes. Here and there by the wayside were the little huts of peasant folks who had to plow and sow the fields and do all the hard work to raise food for their overlords, but who never could own any land themselves or even move away from the wretched places where they lived. The huts were rudely built of clay or wood, and in their doorways little children in bare feet and coarse homespun dresses stood staring at the party riding by. In the fields their brothers, a little older, were working with bent backs beside their fathers, and inside the huts their sisters were helping the mothers weave the coarse cloth for the family clothes, or else were stirring the pots of cabbage soup which was the most any of them had to eat.

"Dear me!" said Alan, "I'm glad I don't have to live like those people!"

"Yes," agreed Henri, "it must be terribly dreary. I guess Father Herluin is right when he says we ought to be glad to learn our lessons and know something, for if we were peasant children we wouldn't have a chance to find out anything! And they have to work all the time just as hard as they can, and never have nice things to eat or wear or any fun like we do, poor things!"

"Look at those washer-women!" said Alan, glancing

with a smile toward a group of women kneeling at he bank of a little stream they were about to cross. "When Count Bertram and the others came along to ford the water the women stated so hard at them that some of the washing is floating off!"

And, sure enough, bobbing up and down with the current, sailed some pieces of linen from the pile of clothes which the women were washing in the stream, pounding them with stones and sousing them up and down just as they do to this day in Normandy.

When the two boys looked back after crossing the ford, the women were wading out with long sticks and pulling back the runaway garments.

Sometimes they passed orchards of apples and pears, and "Oh!" cried Alan, as he sniffed the ripe fruit which the peasants were gathering, "don't it smell good! I wouldn't so much mind being one of those peasants!"

"Yes, you would!" answered Henri, "for you wouldn't dare eat all the apples and pears you wanted! You would have to make most of them into cider for your overlord!"

Now and then, perched on some steep hill, the towers of a tall castle would rise against the sky; and perhaps at the foot of the hill would nestle a little village with gray houses like the village of Noireat.

At mid-day they all stopped in a grassy woodland and

rested the horses and ate some of the food they carried with them.

They rode all afternoon, the road growing steeper and more broken till, toward sunset, it wound down into a picturesque ravine. On either side rose huge rocky crags, and "Look!" cried Henri, gazing up at a lordly castle which crowned one of these. "I wonder what place that is?"

"That is Falaise castle," said one of the squires, who was riding just ahead of Henri and heard his question.

The lad looked with eager interest at the great strong walls and lofty tower looming black against the sunset sky. "Falaise!" he repeated. "Why, then it must be where Duke William was born, and where he rode so fast that night his fool, Goelet, woke him up and warned him to fly!"

"To be sure," said the squire, smiling at Henri's eagerness, "it's the very place. I know this part of the country, for some of my kinsmen live near here. That castle has belonged to the dukes of Normandy for I don't know how many years, but ever and ever so long. And down in the ravine is the town of Falaise; we'll come to it presently. The dukes have always been fond of Falaise, and often come there, though of course they have to live most of the time in the city Rouen where their palace is."

As the lads listened they were all the while riding along, and soon they came to the old town which, as the squire had said, lay for the most part in the ravine. There was a strong wall around it, and when they entered the gate they found themselves in a narrow, crooked street with houses close together on either side. Most of them were built of wood with great timbers showing on the outside, and all had peaked roofs and many gables. Here and there were dark little shops where cloth weavers and leather and metal workers displayed their wares. Everything, of course, was made by hand, for there were no machines for doing things in those days.

Farther along the crooked street they passed the market house, which was open at all sides, only a heavy timber roof upheld by square wooden pillars. Within were many stalls where people sold meat and vegetables, cheese and apples and cider, for Normandy has always been a great place for apples.

As they rode past "I hope they have bought plenty here for the inn where we are to stay tonight," said Henri, "for I am dreadfully hungry!"

"So am I!" replied Alan, for the all day's ride had sharpened their appetites. In a few minutes they came to the inn, a good-sized wooden house built around a courtyard, which they entered through a broad gateway, and soon the landlord was greeting them all, and his servants were leading the knights' horses to stalls while the squires and pages took care of their own.

When they went in for supper the count and his friends were served in a room by themselves, while the others took their luck at the long table spread in the main part of the inn. The air was thick with smoke from a great fireplace where meat was roasting on a spit and the landlord's wife and her maids were making omelettes in long-handled frying pans.

Alan and Henri looked curiously at the other travelers around them as they took their places with a wooden trencher between them. Presently a boy near their own age brought them some meat.

"How do you do?" said Alan, who always liked to make friends with people.

The boy, who had a bright pleasant face, with a friendly look replied to Alan's greeting and then went off to serve some one else. But after supper he came over to the bench where the two pages were sitting, and began to talk to them and to ask them where they came from. When they had answered his questions, they began to ask some themselves.

"What is you name?" Have you always lived in Fal-aise?" inquired Alan. "And what do the boys and girls in town do? Do you go hunting, or to tournaments, or learn to ride or fight? Though I don't quite see how you can in town!"

"My name is Gilles," answered the boy, "and I have always lived here. This is my father's inn, and I help with the work. I can do lots of things, too! I run errands and help wait on the table and I can take care of the horses, and most anything!" he added with an air of pride.

"But what do you do for amusement?! persisted Alan.

"Oh," said Gilles, "we play games, ball and hide and seek, and spin tops and sometimes a puppet show comes to town and we go to that."

"Yes," said Henri, "we do those things at home. I wonder if your puppet shows are like the ones that come to our castle? Last winter a fine one came! The man had a box fixed up like a little stage and a lot of little dolls dressed like different people, and he moved them around with his fingers and pretended to talk for them."

"Yes," put in Alan, "and a couple of them were dressed like knights on horseback and had a regular fight!"

"I saw that one!" said Gilles, with a wise air. "And ever so many others come to Falaise."

"Did you ever go to a tournament?" asked Henri.

"No," answered Gilles vaguely, "I don't know what

that is. But I've been lots of times to the Guibray fair!" he added, his eyes brightening.

It was now the other boys' turn to ask, "What is the Guibray fair?"

"Oh," said Gilles, "it's a big fair the Duke William started in Guibray, a little place up on the hill close to Falaise. There is a fine church there and a shrine with a Madonna that works miracles, and such hundreds and hundreds of pilgrims go there to pray that Duke William thought it would be a fine thing for the Guibray folks to have a fair; so he gave them permission to have one every summer in August, because that's when most of the pilgrims come. It's too bad you didn't get here sooner, for it's been over only about two weeks!"

"What do they do there?" asked Alan.

"Well," answered Gilles, "they have swings, and games, and mistrels and jugglers, and shooting with bows and arrows, and then there are all kinds of things to buy, and more horses and cows than you ever saw!" finished the boy, with round eyes.

Alan and Henri looked rather envious as they heard of the wonders of the Gulbray fair. And, strangely enough, though thus started nearly a thousand years ago, to this day it is still held every August, just as Gilles described it.

As the boys were talking, a little girl went through

the room carrying a doll and a gray kitten. "Is that your sister?" asked Henri of Gilles.

"Yes," answered the lad, "and I have another older one and two brothers."

"What does your sister do? Does she help around the house, too?" asked Henri, for the boys were inquisitive and interested in what kind of lives were led by the boys and girls in town.

"Yes," answered Gilles, "and she is learning to spin and weave, and my older sister can make omelettes and roast meat as well as mother. She don't like to very well, though; she wants to learn to embroider and make things to hang on the wall like some of the rich people in town have. You just ought to see the grand houses some of the rich folks here have! They have chairs that are carved, and wonderful worked cloth hanging on the walls, and some have tiles on their floors, and two of them have kind of holes built in the wall by the fireplace for the smoke to go out! I think they are called chimneys; Duke William's castle has one of them!"

Alan and Henri looked rather blank as they heard of the holes for smoke, which seemed to them quite a fine idea; though we would have laughed at the chimneys Gilles told of, which were really very poor affairs and led the smoke, such of it as went into them, out at the side, not the top of the house.

The two pages, however, said nothing about having none at Noireat, and Alan declared with a lordly air, "Well, I guess Count Bertram has a chair all carved with dragons, and Lady Gisla can embroider tapestries as good as anybody!"

"Where do you go to church?" asked Gilles.

"Why, in the chapel of the castle," answered Henri.

"Well," said Gilles, determined to find something better than their castle had, "I don't believe it's so big as the church of Saint Gervaise here in Falaise! And our church has *glass* in the windows!"

Here the boys' talk was interrupted by the loud ringing of a bell.

"What's that?" asked Alan.

"That's the bell of Saint Gervaise church now!" said Gilles. "It's ringing for curfew!"

"What is curfew?" asked Henri.

"Why," said Gilles in surprise, "don't you know what curfew is? I thought *everybody* knew *that!* We have to cover up our fire with ashes and put out our candles when that bell rings. Duke William ordered it, and father says it's to make people careful that their houses don't burn down at night when everybody's asleep, and that it's to make folks go to bed early, too, and keep out of mischief."

"Well, I guess it's meant more for you town people," said Alan. "There are more of you to get into mischief! And your wooden houses would burn down quicker than stone castles, too." But Gilles had already run to help his father heap ashes over the glowing logs still smoldering in the fireplace, and all the travelers in the room began to find places on the floor or benches where they might pass the night. Alan and Henri and the squires of Count Bertram's party stretched themselves out wherever they could, and soon everybody was asleep.

CHAPTER XI
WAITING FOR THE WIND

The two pages washed their faces next morning at the well in the courtyard, and after an early breakfast mounted their ponies and rode off with Count Bertram and the others.

All day they rode, and at nightfall came to a pretty little stream. It was the river Dives, and close by was a village where the party passed the night in an inn much like that of Falaise, only smaller and smokier.

The next day they followed the stream till late in the afternoon, when as last it spread out through flat meadow lands and by and by emptied into the sea near the old town of Dives where Duke William was waiting for his forces to gather.

"Oh, look!" cried Henri, who was gazing eagerly ahead. "Do you suppose that long white line is the sea?"

"Yes!" said Alan, with equal eagerness. "And yonder must be the town of Dives." And then, as they came still nearer, "Oh, see the ships! And all the tents and flags and horses!"

Everybody urged on their horses, and soon they had reached the gathering place and were looking about with wonder at the throng of soldiers, and stir and bustle everywhere going on. Every inn and house in the town of Dives was full, and of the hosts who had come to join Duke William, far the greater number were camped in the tents pitched in the grassy meadows between the town and the sea.

Everywhere flags and pennons were fluttering, and so many war horses were grazing in the meadows that Henri, laughing, said to Alan, "I guess if Gilles could see all those he wouldn't think so much of that Guibray fair!"

"No!" cried Alan. "And wouldn't his eyes get round if he could get a glimpse of those ships!" And Alan's own eyes grew very round indeed as he gazed at the bright colored sails crowding the mouth of the river and gleaming in the distance along the edge of the sea.

Count Bertram and his friends soon arranged for some tents, and the party went into camp like the others. Alan and Henri ran errands and helped all they could; and though they were tired out when dark fell, they were so excited they could hardly sleep when not long after sunset all the camp-fires were covered up and quiet fell over the town and meadow.

The fires were all promptly covered, for Duke William

himself was hard by in a great timbered house which he had caused to be built months before near the river bank, as he needed a comfortable place in which to stay while he attended to the building of his fleet.

The next morning the two pages went to look at Duke William's house (which is still standing), and found it very large and attractive.

"I wonder if that is Duke William's device?" said Henri, pointing to a carved stone lion holding his paw on a shield and looking down at them from the gateway.

"Yes," said some one standing near, "that is, part of it. You know the duke's device is three lions, the same as on the flag of Normandy; and if you stay here a little while, you will probably see Duke William himself. He generally comes out about this time."

The boys ventured inside the open gateway and into the courtyard; the house, built around this, had a peaked roof and many gables and dormer windows, and around the second story ran a wooden balcony with a flight of steps leading to the courtyard.

Presently a door opened from one of the rooms facing the balcony, and a man stepped out and came down the stairway and through the courtyard.

He was followed by several knights and pages, and

when one of the latter passed near Alan, "Is that Duke William?" he hurriedly whispered.

"Yes," answered the page, as he scampered on after the others.

Alan and Henri followed, too, all the while looking hard at the duke whenever they got a chance. He was a tall, handsome man, strong and powerfully built; he had a high forehead, and his hair and small mustache were both closely cropped; but, though little over forty years old, his face showed stern, careworn lines, for Duke William's life had been full of struggles and he had been obliged to fight his way from babyhood up.

"He looks like a duke,—don't you think so, Alan?" asked Henri.

"Yes, indeed!" said Alan. "And he is splendidly dressed, too, only I thought he would have on the crimson velvet mantle and big crown that Master Herve said dukes wear."

"Well," said Henri wisely, "I don't suppose he wants to wear those things while he is attending to his army out here. I think he looks much better in what he has on."

The boys kept following the ducal party at a respectful distance, and watched with interest as Duke William went down to the water's edge and began looking over the boats.

"They look a good deal like the dragon ships Herve told us Rolf the Ganger came in," said Alan, "only they aren't so gayly painted as he said those were."

"No," said Henri, "and I guess they are some bigger than his. But they have the red and blue sails, and long rows of oars, and are all curved up high at the ends and carved just like Herve said. I don't see any dragons, but there are some with heads carved on them!"

"I see two dragons!" cried Alan, as with keen eyes he searched the high prows of the hundreds of long narrow ships crowding the river.

As the boys watched, great quantities of salted meat and other provisions were stored on those of the ships that were set apart to carry supplies; and baggage and tents and weapons of all kinds were loaded on others. For Duke William expected to set sail within a week at most.

But though all the soldiers gathered and all was ready, still the ships floated quietly at the mouth of the river Dives; for there was no wind to swell the sails and carry them toward Britain. The long oars alone were not enough to take the heavily loaded vessels without the aid of sails, and no one then had even dreamed of such as thing as a steam-boat.

Duke William and all the fighting men grew more and more impatient as windless day after day passed by

THE SHIPS FLOATED QUIETLY AT THE
MOUTH OF THE RIVER DIVES.

till almost two weeks were gone. But though everybody else anxiously watched and waited for the wind, Alan and Henri could not help but be secretly glad of the delay. For as they were not old enough to go along, they knew that just as soon as the fleet sailed they would have to go back to Noireat, which would be very lonely and quiet. Count Bertram had arranged for them to return home with some young squires from one of the neighboring castles.

CHAPTER XII

The Duchess Matilda's Gift

"Dear me!" said Alan one day, while still the ships waited for the wind, "won't it seem tame to go back to Noireat after being here so long?"

"Yes, indeed!" said Henri, with a sigh. "We surely will miss seeing all these knights and soldiers every day, and all the horses and ships! And then at night, the fire in the castle won't be half so much fun as the camp-fires here, even if they are put out early. And the stories the men have to tell about the wars they have been in beat old Herve's!"

"No," said Alan, "I don't think they are better than Master Herve's, but they are different. And then the minstrels here, what good songs they sing! I didn't expect though to find any of *them* in camp! I didn't know they ever went to war!"

"Oh, yes!" said Henri, "I heard one of the knights say that the minstrels, when they wanted to, could fight as well as anybody. But Duke William's minstrel, Talifer, is going along just to sing his war songs so as to cheer on the men. And the knight said that Talifer is so brave and that he sings so well that he will probably ride right in front of everybody!"

"He certainly sings well!" agreed Alan. "You know the other day when we passed Duke William's house, what a beautiful song we heard Talifer singing!"

Here the talk of the boys was cut short as Count Bertram called them to do some errand and they quickly sprang up to obey him.

The next morning Henri awakened with a sigh; for there was a gusty sound without and the flap of the tent had blown open.

"Do you hear that?" he asked, nudging Alan who slept beside him.

"Yes," said Alan, dolefully rubbing his eyes, "it's that old wind!"

Soon it was blowing strongly, and though not quite in the direction wanted, Duke William decided to go along the Norman coast to a point a little nearer Britain; so off the ships sailed to the seaport town of Saint Valery.

Alan and Henri were very disconsolate as they watched the last sail fade away at the rim of the sky.

"Oh, don't you wish we were on one of those ships!" cried Alan longingly.

"Indeed I do!" answered Henri. "It seems lonesome

already! It wouldn't be half so much fun staying here with the soldiers all gone, and I'd just as soon go back home!"

"Yes," said Alan, "but we can't right away, for one of the squires of the party we are to go with told me a while ago that his brother, Jean, is sick and they don't want to leave him alone here, so we are all to wait a few days till he gets better."

"Well," said Henri, "I don't see where we will stay, for the camps are all broken up."

"Oh," said Alan, "I forgot to say the squire has arranged for us all to go over to Duke William's house. There are a couple of small rooms the care-taker will let us have, and his wife will get our meals."

"Who will pay for us?" asked Henri.

"Oh, I don't know," answered Alan, "But I suppose Count Bertram will fix it all right when he comes back."

So the little party moved over to Duke William's house, where the sick squire, Jean, was made comfortable and soon began to improve under the nursing of the care-taker's wife.

As Henri had said, everything seemed very quiet and deserted after the sailing of the fleet. But though at first the boys hardly knew what to do with themselves, they soon found plenty of entertainment in wandering about the old town and along the edge of the sea, which was a never ending wonder to them.

Thus several days passed; and then one morning word came to Dives that the fleet was again becalmed at Saint Valery, waiting vainly for favoring winds. At this news one of the young squires exclaimed, "Let us ride over to Saint Valery! I don't believe it is so very far away, and I think by hard riding we could reach it in a day. Let us go over and see what they are doing there!"

"All right!" cried the others eagerly, and "May we go, too?" Henri made haste to ask.

"Yes," said the squire, "we'll all go! Jean is better, and the care-takers will look after him till we get back."

So, getting their horses and ponies ready as quickly as possible, off they started for Saint Valery.

It proved to be a three days' ride instead of one, but youth and good spirits, and a little money they managed to muster, carried them through, and it was a tired but happy little party that reached Saint Valery at nightfall the third day. Wrapping their riding cloaks about them, they lay down on the ground and slept soundly till morning.

When they awakened, they found much the same scene as had been at Dives. Tents and soldiers, knights and war-horses and ships, and great numbers of the people of Saint Valery coming and going among the throng.

The two pages had some trouble finding Count Bertram and Hugh among so many, but at last they did.

"Ho!" said Count Bertram, staring at them in surprise, "where did you young rascals drop from? I though you were home by this time!"

He smiled when the boys hurriedly explained to him how they had come. "Well, well," he said, "I am glad enough to see you and only wish I could take you along! Meantime you can make yourselves useful here."

And he and Hugh between them soon found a number of things for them to do.

So ten days more passed. Then at last the east wind came.

Oh, what rejoicing there was then among all those warriors! And what a hurrying and scurrying to get back in the ships everything that has been taken ashore during the long wait! Horses neighed and whinnied and pranced as they were being led aboard, silken banners and pennons were set flying from every mast, men in armor, men with cross-bows, glittering spears and lances and shining battle-axes, all were crowded on the long ships, as the sun shone and sparkled and the people on shore ran to and fro bringing this and that thing to the water's edge.

Then all at once some one noticed a strange ship on

the horizon. Its curving, gayly colored sails gleamed bright and billowy in the brilliant morning light as faster and faster it sped into the harbour of Saint Valery. And then, nearing the fleet, proudly it came to shore just as everything was ready and Duke William was about to embark on the ship he had chosen for his own.

As the people gazed at the beautiful new vessel, so much finer that any there, a great shout of admiration went up. "The *Mora!*" they cried, reading the name painted in bright colors on the side of the ship. And then on the flag, waving from the top of the mast, they saw embroidered the three lions of Normandy, and "The duke's ship!" everybody shouted.

But Duke William himself was staring at it in utter bewilderment. He stared at its beautiful shape, as its lion flag, and, most of all, he stared at the carved and gilded figure-head at its high prow. For this was the image of no other than his own little son William, his name-sake and favorite child. The golden boy grasped in one hand a bow and arrow, and with the other held to his lips an ivory trumpet which he seemed in the act of blowing.

As Duke William stood, the picture of amazement, a richly clad lady was seen near the mast of the ship, and in another moment his lips parted in a joyful smile as

"The Duchess Matilda! Hurrah, hurrah!" burst from a thousand throats about him.

It was indeed the Duchess Matilda, who as a surprise for the duke, had ordered the beautiful new ship built for his special use, and she had come with it because she wanted to have the pleasure of presenting it to him herself.

As for Duke William, he was overjoyed, and declared the gallant way in which the *Mora* had sailed into harbor was a good omen for his undertaking. At once he ordered all his own things taken from the ship he had meant to use and placed on the fine new one.

When once more all was ready, and Duke William had taken leave of Duchess Matilda, and every one had said good-by to their friends, the anchors were drawn up, the sails set for Britain, music played, people cheered and shouted, and away went the fleet and the fearless army which was to help Duke William earn the name of "the Conqueror" and win for him the crown of Britain.

Alan and Henri, standing at the edge of the water, shaded their eyes with their hands and looked and looked as the countless swelling sails fluttered out to sea. And as the last gleam from the *Mora* faded from sight, they fancied that from the ivory horn of the golden boy upon its prow there echoed back a brave "Good-by!—Good-by!"